SOPHIA'S GARDEN

A Journey of a Little Girl Looking for Heaven

Angie Wilson

ISBN 979-8-89345-580-9 (paperback)
ISBN 979-8-89345-581-6 (digital)

Christian Faith Publishing
832 Park Avenue
Meadville, PA 16335
www.christianfaithpublishing.com

Printed in the United States of America

PREFACE

When I first learned I was going to be a hospice nurse, I was nonchalant. It was temporary to me—a short-term career move so that my children would not have to go to day care. My husband teased me, saying I wouldn't last a year. He literally shook his head in disbelief when we discussed that I was accepting the hospice role. I was a first responder in my community, a healer, a nurse that fixed things fueled by adrenaline. Little did I know I was living out a plan designed for me and finding my ministry.

My first hospice role was a night-call nurse. I promise you I would not have survived those years without adrenaline. They were the best and the worst times of my nursing years. I went out day or night for admissions and emergencies and when people passed away. I traveled highways, gravel roads, and dirt roads. Rain, sleet, and snow are understatements. One night, the county maintainer got me to a patient in need during a blizzard. Another night a deputy met me and safely disarmed a veteran experiencing terminal restlessness. He fought hard in his final days, and I will never forget him and the painful journey that he relived as he began leaving this world. He did find comfort and peace before he left this world.

I was also a teacher or a navigator for patients and their caregivers to help them see the future through the unknown and believe that they could indeed do what was thrust on them during this unspeakable impending loss they were experiencing. I soon learned that healing did not require a cure. I also learned there is more to managing a patient's needs than medical testing and medications.

I also learned to appreciate what I was experiencing. I learned to share the stories. I learned to grieve the losses that I, too, was feeling. I learned to listen. Every person had a story, and I needed to meet them where they were at, placing my personal feelings aside so that I could walk alongside of them, supporting them to take next steps as they prepared for goodbye or "see you later."

Finally, I learned that though dying may be difficult, it doesn't have to be without celebration when there is faith and hope. I promise there is still grieving, but that is us experiencing the void where there has been the gift and earthly presence of love. I have been blessed to have had the front-row seat of heaven's waiting room and have been able to witness the awe and beauty that so many have shared as they leave this world to enter the next.

My hope is that this story helps you navigate your journey, whether that be yourself or as a care-giver to your loved one.

I wish you peace and comfort and a special thanks for inviting me into your journey.

Much love.
XOXO, Angie Wilson.

ACKNOWLEDGMENTS

My forever love and thanks to my husband, Todd. He has been my best friend, confidant, and anchor through all the ups and downs in life. He has spoken the truth when I needed to hear it, and he has held my hand in silence when there were no words. He makes me laugh every day and is the best cheerleader a woman can have. His fierce, quiet faith has taught me more than I can express. He understands and participates in my longing to live every moment as robustly as possible as none of us knows what tomorrow will bring. He believes in me always. This book would not be here without him. I love you, Wilson.

To my boys, Luke and Josh, who have grown up in a home where death and dying is a daily conversation. They grew up knowing Mom on the phone was in immediate silence because I had to talk privately to a patient or family in distress. Also knowing at times, they knew I needed to leave their ball games suddenly to help someone. They never once complained. They volunteered for hospice and visited patients. I have watched them both grow into men with the same quiet faith as their dad and with an empathy and caregiving that melts this mama's heart. Love you always, Luke Man and Lil Guy.

To the girls who chose my sons and the moms of our beautiful grandchildren. They and our grandchildren have completed our family and filled the holes we didn't know we had. They are beautiful souls and our blessings. I love you and love that you chose us to love.

Hello, Sophia!

"Hi! I have something for your garden. My grandma told me you love to plant flowers and be in your garden."

"I picked out these succulents for you," she said, drawing out the word *succulent*. "Because you don't succ—or suck!"

We laughed and laughed.

"Sophia, I love laughing with you. You are one of the best parts of my day!"

"They are making a garden for me out back."

"I love gardens. Tell me about yours."

"It is getting really big, and there is so much purple. We are getting lights too!"

Sophia looked away.

"Sophia, you're quiet now. What are you thinking about?"

"Who will take care of the garden when I am gone?"

"Are you worried about what will happen to your garden?"

"I love my garden. I don't want to leave it. My family and dogs will visit the garden, and I won't be there. They say I am going to heaven to be with Jesus and my grandparents, but I don't really understand, and I don't want to go alone or leave my family and friends. And my dogs, I don't want to leave my dogs." Sophia pet her pup as she talked.

"I have never been to heaven, but I have been with people who are getting ready to go to heaven. So many have told me what they see. I have also had some incredible dreams. I feel like I get to have had a window to heaven that leaves me feeling so good and excited about heaven. Can I share some stories with you?"

Sophia looked up with a faint but guarded smile and said, "Yes, I want to hear about heaven. Please tell me some stories."

"Alright, sweet girl, I will share some beautiful stories with you about the glimpses I have had of heaven."

THE
STORIES
AND
DREAMS OF
HEAVEN

DORIS'S DOOR

I had the absolute pleasure of caring for my Aunt Doris Ann as she was making her way to heaven. I had just given her a bath—she was sleeping most of the time. She really was not talking. Today was no different. She did not open her eyes once. However, she did manage to whisper to me. She was telling me she could see a door. She spoke of being nervous and uncertain about the door and if she should open it. We held hands in silence. I could smell her fresh coconut lotion, and her pale clean skin was beautiful next to her bright-red nightgown. My cousins bantered and told funny stories in the background. I rubbed my thumb over her red fingernails.

"Tell me about the door, Aunt DA."

"It's a big door," she said slowly and drawn out.

"What makes you uncertain about the door?" I asked.

She took many deep breaths. "Oh, it's a good door, I know it is." She spoke slow and deliberate and with a breathy voice.

I asked her why she didn't want to open the door. She explained to me that she wasn't sure if she deserved to open it. She spoke of worry about what if she opened it, and it was a bad place. I reassured her and reminded her that she spoke of the door being good.

"What do you believe is on the other side?"

"A party and a celebration," she said.

As she rested, we spoke about the parties she had thrown. She loved a gathering. She loved to be in the spotlight at the party. We then spoke of feasts and celebrations in heaven and how I imagined them to be. She opened her eyes and looked at me out of the corner of her eye, maybe a bit disbelieving. I grinned at her.

I also reassured her that I truly believed that there would be a table set for a king and feasts. I was reminded of a song that I love that has the lyrics "Come to the Table." I reminded DA that she loved everyone around the table. I was teasing her as well as she used to hide a tape recorder so she could listen to the conversations long after the party had ended. I reassured her that it would be the best party and feast she had ever been to. She smiled and rested with a simple nod of approval.

I told her that when she was ready, she had my permission to go through the door. She spoke just a few more words in the few days that followed. She then found her way through the door. On her terms, just like she lived her life.

X's and O's

I met an incredible farmer once. He lived on a gravel road and was the only house you could see for miles. One cold snowy night in February, he told his wife and children that tonight was the night he would be going to heaven. His physical body didn't seem to match that statement, and his daughters became quite concerned that maybe he was hallucinating or needed to be checked, so I arrived to see him. He pointed out the picture window in his living room toward his fields that were empty and covered with snow. It was so cold and dark. There were hundreds of stars in the sky, and the moon was reflecting on the snow. Over the next few hours, he made many statements that described what he was seeing. Once he exclaimed, "*Look!* The crops are so wonderful." Another time, he described the flowers, "They are the most beautiful that I have ever seen!" As we took our gaze to the window he was passionately pointing at, the fields were frozen and bare.

"What color is that?" he asked. "I don't even know that color or kind of flower," he exclaimed.

He described the pastures and flowers in detail. He spoke of what a miraculous and bountiful harvest it would be. He was overwhelmed with joy and emotion but speaking softly and tenderly. He then went on to describe the people. During this time, he would rest and then open his eyes and attempt to make eye contact with his family but could only look past them. I told the family that I believed him and tonight could very well be the night. I suggested saying goodbyes and embracing this glimpse of heaven that he was giving us.

He sent his daughter to retrieve a gift that he had stored away for his wife. It was a beautiful piece of jewelry. The pendants were *X*'s and *O*'s. He kissed his wife's hand as he placed the jewelry in her hand and said, "If you are missing me, wear this to be reminded of our love. This will be my hug and kiss for you from heaven." He rested again as his loved ones crawled into bed with him and said their goodbyes. It was the most beautiful peaceful time. He gasped in excitement at one point, "Oh! There is Joe and Maxine, and there is Mel! I see so many, there is Chad and Leo. Look over there, it is Mike and Mason!" He was so excited to see these people, and although he was whispering and weak and it was spread out over several minutes, you could feel the energy and pure joy that he was experiencing. I learned from his family that these names were all people he knew, and all had passed away. Some more than thirty years ago. He soon closed his eyes to rest and then finished his journey to heaven. We knew in that moment that each of those people were there to greet him and take him home to the beautiful harvest.

YELLOW BIRD

I love birds, especially yellow birds. From the tropical drink that I shared with my sister off the coast of the Bahamas to the goldfinches in my garden, my affinity for these birds has only grown. I first learned how to attract goldfinches from a sweet patient of mine. He had ALS and was unable to move his upper body. He sat at the window in his kitchen for hours watching the birds. He had thistle sacks all over his yard, and the goldfinches swarmed the thistle. Since that time, my husband and I have had such pleasure watching the finches in our yard.

Fast-forward several years to a time where I had the absolute pleasure of taking care of a lovely young woman. She was very quiet, a woman of very little words. Leaving this world for the next was very private to her. In her final days, she also proved to be very strong. One night, after she had been in bed for over twenty-four hours, seeming to be in her very last hours, she came walking down the hall on her cell phone with her credit card, placing an order for pizza. Her son had arrived. It had been a distant and difficult relationship with no recent visits. Her family was shocked. I encouraged them to let her do this; she was making a gesture as a mom, to feed him one last meal. Although she didn't say it, it was clear she wanted to break bread with him, and that is just what she did.

As we spoke and shared more stories, we learned that morning she had a similar experience with her daughter that had arrived from out of town. Only this time, she insisted that her daughter get out of bed and have coffee with her. Again, she had not been out of bed much and had not been eating or drinking. And that day, they shared one last cup of coffee at the kitchen table together. In this home, the table was the hub for all family gatherings and prep for meals. It was a gathering place for moms and daughters, sisters, and friends. A few months earlier, in her final weeks, she had planned a picnic where she prepared all the food. She refused any help. This brought frustration and concern to her mom and daughter, who were her primary caregivers, as they knew she was quite weak. They wanted to help her so much and did not want to let her down. During this moment, preparing and serving food for her family, it became very clear this was her final gift to her loved ones. She needed to independently go through this ritual of caring for her loved ones and prepare them this last meal.

The next hours and day were very quiet for her, sleeping with some laboring but very aware and alert. During this time, she told me that there was a man outside her window. She nodded toward the window. As I looked out the window to the empty pasture, I said, "Tell me about the man."

"I don't know him, but I know he is here to stand watch for me. I trust him and want him near," she said.

I received a simple nod when I asked her if he was part of her journey home. Another nod when I asked if she was glad that he was present. Later, I checked on her again.

"Do you see the yellow bird?" she asked.

I explained to her that I did not see the bird but wanted to hear about it. She was tired, and words were sparse, but she explained it was flying all around her. She had a slight smile as she described the bird. She tried to follow the bird with her eyes. She had a peace. No grimacing or moaning. There is a labor that can happen at this time, and this seemed done as she was just resting.

I stepped away and told her mom about the yellow bird. Her mom was even more stoic and fierce than the patient, a warrior that I admired. I got the familiar nod with these words, "It won't be long now."

Before I left, I shared with this lovely young woman that I had grown to look forward to our visits that her mom said it wouldn't be long now since the yellow bird was here. That was the last visit with her. Some say a yellow bird's presence may symbolize angels visiting or even a spirit guide; others believe something positive is about to happen. In hospice, we speak about a belief that birds symbolize the passing between this world and the next world.

JESUS LOVES ME

Mike loved his family, and they loved him. This was shown to him in the care and presence of his family at this incredible time of his life. Mike had been proud of his career. His work had required a great deal of physical labor, so rest was hard for him. He wanted to work hard and provide for his family. He felt guilty for being sick and leaving his family sooner than he had imagined this time in his life to be. He worried that maybe he had not done enough for his family. He also loved having fun and playing around with his family. As he became weaker and his illness advanced, he also became more anxious. He wasn't sure about going to heaven. Some people are worried that they don't deserve heaven. I believe he was fighting those hours and minutes of calm and rest that we often see before our loved ones go to heaven. He wasn't so sure that was his next place.

When he was in his final hours, he thrashed and moved and resisted rest and comfort. He worked as hard as he ever had in his life. This lasted for three days and three nights. He was tired. His family was tired. We made sure everyone came to see him and tell him goodbye. We made sure that his favorite stories were told, and fun was had with card games near him so he could enjoy the fun as well. We made sure his pastor had been there to help with closure. The work continued, and the thrashing continued. We eventually gave him some alone time with the person who had been with him his entire life, through thick and thin, his caretaker from his youth, his big sister.

She crawled into his king-sized beautiful bed and snuggled him, like she did when they were small children. She whispered to him, reminisced about their childhood, their hopes, and fears. She held him and rocked him. Siblings that were in their later years now and had not had a moment like this since childhood. Eventually, his thrashing lessened but was still present. His big sister said, "Remember the song we used to sing when we were scared?"

Mike had not spoken in days, and he said, "*Yes!*" as loudly and fiercely as I had ever heard him speak. And together at that moment, they sang "Jesus Loves Me." Quietly, softly, broken at times with tears. As they did this, his anxiety was gone; his angered, wrinkled forehead softened; and he smiled weakly but beautifully. He quit thrashing and held his family's hands as they told him it was okay to go to heaven. He made his way to heaven in the next few hours with all his loved ones on that king-size bed with him. It was truly beautiful and peaceful.

MARC'S MIRACLE

Marc was an amazing man. I had known him most of my life. Strong. Fierce. Risk-taker. Wildly independent. Authentic. Passionate. Driven by faith. Husband. Dad. Grandpa. Friend. Pastor. Real. So many qualities and attributes all packaged up in one human. When I found out I was going to be caring for him, I was concerned. First, he was kind of famous in our neck of the woods. Second, I heard those words, "But you can't talk about dying with him." Hmm. That's why I am going to see him. There is no cure.

So we started our journey together. I hadn't seen him since he was back from Africa. I had heard he was intensely more spiritual and passionate than he had ever been. The first time I saw him, he was lying in his living room. And his eyes. Holy moly, his eyes. They pierced me to my soul. I can't describe it, but all these years later, not only do I still see it, but I also still feel it. Some days I just think about it so that I can feel it again. If you were there, you know, you just know. At the time, I didn't realize the full gravity of it, and honestly, maybe I still don't. Anyway, this side of heaven, I don't.

So I visited, worked on his comfort, danced around what I saw. He was dying. Every visit, our first few words were the same. "Hi, Marc, what's the most important thing I can do for you today?"

He would grin and say, "First, how is your relationship with Jesus?"

We could not move to his care until my spiritual well-being was tucked in. Each and every visit. Early on, we both made concessions to one another. I would blur every professional hospice boundary and talk about my personal faith and relationship with Jesus, and I would save my trump card of calling in everyone to say goodbye and talk about death until I felt we were at the finish line.

You see, Marc didn't believe that he was going to leave his earthly body and go to heaven. He was going to be a miracle that went to heaven and came back to share what he saw and proclaim the gospel. Honestly, it seemed out of this world, unimaginable to me, but I met him where he was. I began to really look forward to our visits. He filled my cup. There was a rawness to his spirituality that I had never seen or experienced. I hope I filled his cup too. We tried everything, and still, his earthly body was becoming weaker and frailer. All the bodily functions were not doing their jobs any longer, and I knew where we were.

I will never forget this day. That fierce light in his eyes was dimmer. I was down on my knees on the floor saying it was time. I was playing my trump card and calling in his kiddos to come be at his bedside. And do you know what he said? "How is your relationship with Jesus?"

I grinned and told him my answer. We quietly and swiftly moved to the next steps. I helped his family call in the kids. I worked on Marc's comfort. We comforted those around Marc who had been praying for a miracle. We held the phone for people to say goodbye. It was beautiful.

I told him that sometimes miracles don't happen on earth. Some won't experience their miracle until they get to heaven. I explained I believed he was still the miracle he spoke of, but it might just look differently to those of us still here on earth. He nodded. He knew he was on the cusp of his miracle. He went to heaven that evening.

He will forever be a miracle to me and to so many others. I often wonder what he saw in Africa. Someone told me, "I think Marc saw the face of God and could not stay on earth any longer." That truly resonated with me, and I still think about that as a possibility. For sure, he was part of a miracle, just like Marc said. But maybe we were looking at the miracle from the wrong direction. Africa is where his journey began as a miracle worker, then he came back to the States to proclaim the gospel of what he had learned and lived. At the end of the day, he truly was a miracle who touched so many. Me included.

ANGELIC DAVID

When we think about our experiences and the ages at which they happened, it is remarkable to think about how that shapes your future self. David is that for me. When I was in middle school, my cousin David suddenly died. He was fun, loving…what some would call wild and nonconforming. I even heard him called bad. He wasn't bad to me. He was kind and gentle. I was drawn to him. It was the time of landline telephones, and if a phone rang in the middle of the night, it was never good news. I remember the phone ringing somewhere around two or three in the morning. I heard whispering, and I knew my parents were up. My grandma had been ill, so I was sure she was back in the hospital. When I got up in the morning, my mom was sitting at the table in the dark with my dad. They had clearly been crying. I had seen my mom cry but never my dad. I pushed and pushed to find out what was wrong, and they said it was nothing for me to worry about and wanted me to go to school. If I was nothing, I was persistent. My mom eventually told me that my cousin had died during the night from a drug overdose.

What? How? I had just seen him. We had taken a ton of pictures of five generations. I have the best memories of him. Once, he was recording a song off the radio with his cassette player because that is what we did then, before Alexa and Spotify. He was recording "Fly Like an Eagle" by the Steve Miller Band. We had to sit very quietly because every sound would be picked up by the recorder. I had been previously scolded for this by him. As we sat cross-legged on the floor in the basement, he replayed it after it was done recording and sang along. It was beautiful to me.

Another time, many years prior to our basement recording studio, we were at our great-grandma's house. For me, this was a time that memories were beginning to stick in detail. Sunday dinner was still a glorious thing that you didn't miss. We all met at Grandma Beason's small in-town house that came to be her home when she left the farm. Fried chicken, mashed potatoes, and all the feel-goods were part of those Sundays. There were three channels on TV, and on Sundays at noon was wrestling. Grandma loved it, and we all gathered around the little TV and watched. On this day, I crawled all over David, begging him to chase me. There was no chasing to be done in the tiny space, but we did crawl all over and pretend to be bears and growled and growled. I remember the adults laughing, and they couldn't believe how David was playing with me. We eventually settled down and watched TV while I leaned on him. It truly is my favorite memory of him.

When he died, I was old enough to know the finality of it and aware of my own mortality. Sudden death brings so many emotions. My parents made decisions for me that truly impact how I present things today to those facing loss. I had to go to school that day while my parents packed up and headed to support my aunt. That was tough and very lonely. Somewhere along the way, it was also decided that I would go to school instead of attending the funeral. Also tough and even more lonely. I didn't get to say goodbye, I didn't get to be at the cemetery while all the cousins were doing cousin things. I was mad. Really mad. I share that experience now with others when they are questioning what role and activities their children should participate in. It is so individualized, but so important to look at all options and find the child's comfort level and needs. I know my parents believed they were making the best decision for me and for them through their grief.

Days turned to weeks, and I grappled with David's death. We didn't talk about it. I can't be sure how long it was, but sometime in the months after his death, I had a vivid dream. It was short, sweet, slow, and over too quickly. I can still visualize it today. David was standing there surrounded by light. His hair was still long, but wispier and flowing. It was like there was a breeze, but there wasn't one. He was wearing the brightest white clothes. He was so bright that I couldn't look at him for long periods of time. He told me he was safe and happy, and I shouldn't worry. His smile was fierce and gentle and kind and soft and perfect. He was peaceful. No harsh edges, No sadness in his eyes. I felt peace as well. That was my first experience that shaped me and gave me the goggles I needed to be a hospice nurse. I just didn't know it yet, but it was at the beginning of my journey.

COACH

Do you ever have one of those dreams that is so vivid and so real, with bright colors and lights, but everything around you is moving and you're not? Like outer space or driving in a snowstorm with the snowflakes zooming by you, but you don't care because you are so excited to be in the moment, watching in awe. I had one of those dreams. I was alone at a golf club, and this gentleman walked up and sat beside me. It was Coach, one of the most influential mentors from my youth. I honestly hadn't thought about him in a long time, and out of the blue one night, he was there, next to me at the club of a golf course I had never been to.

There was this panoramic view of the golf course. I could see all around us. Everything was zooming and moving, and I couldn't really see it all. I knew there were people there, but I couldn't see them. I couldn't take my eyes off him or the view, but I didn't care. I wanted to take it in; it was as if I knew the time was short. It was so lush and green. It was bright and sunny and seemed to be raining at the same time, and although we were inside, it felt like we were outside. Kind of like if a golf course and the garden of Eden had a baby! It was frankly the most incredible golf course that I have ever seen. It went on and on.

It was so wonderful to see him. He was young and tan with signature grayish hair. We each had a mug of ice-cold beer. Sweat was running down the mugs. He was sipping. He was smiling. He had his well-known grin while looking down, yet also looking up at me. It felt so good. So comfortable. He told me he was proud of me. We spoke of leadership and coaching and how they are the same. I explained how hard it was some days. He said, "Keep going, keep growing. You are making a difference." And as easy as the dream came, it drifted away. Slow and easy.

That week, I had to travel for work. Lots of windshield time. It was a "hurry up and wait" kind of week. I couldn't shake the dream. It was so real and still so clear. It wasn't fading like dreams do. It became nagging and wouldn't leave me alone. Like someone poking me to be annoying. I finally reached out to my friend, his daughter, and told her about my dream. She listened and went on to tell me that she was at the bedside of her father-in-law, and he was in his final hours. We chatted about her current circumstances and how she was "loving him to heaven," which I thought was a beautiful way to describe the part of the journey they were in. She told me that when her dad had died, his last days were so difficult. Right now, at this time when her father-in-law was passing, she had been surrounded with her grief and thoughts of those distressing hours of her dad's last days. She had not really thought about what his heaven would be like. Her words to me were, "I needed your dream to get my memory back of what his heaven is."

My husband tells everyone that he has been in hospice for just shy of thirty years. And really, that is the truth. He has conversations that other husbands don't have just because of my life's work. Death and dying are normalized in our home. We debrief, and he talks me off the ledge, cheers me on, and stands next to me when we run into a family that is in a sea of grief and loss. Plain and simple, I would not be able to do this line of work without him. When I dreamed about Coach, Todd and I sat in our garage and talked about it. We spoke about glimpses of heaven and the incredible experiences I have had while walking and working on holy ground. We imagined if Coach picked us to be his rest stop on his journey through to help guide a loved one home, his daughter's father-in-law. If maybe he picked us because he knew we would believe and share. I don't know, but I do have faith, and I hope so. I hope that part of my purpose is to share these experiences to help others' faith blossom along the way.

THE CABIN

Robb came into our lives as a loud, rowdy teen with a heart as big as the moon. He made us laugh. He drove us bonkers. He was wild, kind, funny, caring, devoted, a friend to many, stubborn, and first and foremost, a husband, a dad, and a grandpa. We all grew up and eventually grew older together. I had the pleasure of caring for Robb's sister-in-law. Because of that relationship, Robb and I spoke about dying, family, forgiveness, and all the dynamics of life and death. The night she died, Robb and I shared a moment across a full gym and an eventual hug that I will never forget. We were in a gym full of our friends and their kids for a celebration, and we were the only two with hearts breaking and tears flowing. We didn't speak and did our best to put on the parent face for the night.

When we got the text message that Robb had suddenly died, I was right back in that moment where we spoke about heaven and dying. Our world was rocked. What? How? He was larger than life; there was no way that he was called home to heaven. *This has got to be lies*. With great sadness, we came to realize it was very true. Funerals and visitations came and went, and my husband and I still looked for Robb where we both saw him every single school morning. He wasn't there. We missed that wave, that smile, the raunchy jokes, that security knowing he was making sure the kiddos in our community were safe.

One night, my husband told me, "I saw Robb, and I heard Robb plain as day." My first reaction was, "*Where?* Oh man, I have missed him!" Then reality hit that he wasn't here with us. Todd went on to explain that he had a dream. My husband does not dream, ever. And on the rare time that he does, he can't remember one detail and just remembers maybe that he had one. He then told me about his dream.

"I dreamed that you and I stumbled across a cabin. You wanted to check it out, so we headed for the steps and the door loudly flew open before we could take those steps. There stood Robb, grinning ear to ear! 'Round guy, you want a beer?' The cabin was old. It was simple. It was off the grid, in the timber. Just like where we would expect Robb to be."

He had a few people with him. No one that we knew, but they were all laughing and talking, sharing drinks and stories. Just like always, the dream was fast and furious; and just like that, the dream was done.

As Todd told me his dream, we always go back to that same old conversation. Was Robb visiting, letting us know he was home? Is this Robb's heaven? It was for sure one of his happy places on earth. That dream came when I was struggling to find the words to tell my sweet friend Sophia about heaven. I told her about the big, tall, gentle giant of a man that is always smiling at her school. The one that set out the crossing signs every morning to keep everyone safe. I explained that he went to heaven before her. As we talked, she said she would know to look for him, and he would help her cross the road one more time.

Thanks, Robb, for visiting Todd. You helped me to help a sweet little girl. I know you knew we would listen, and yet you would not want this attention of being a part of helping; you just would want all the kiddos to be cared for. Cheers, Robb!

UNCLE RANDY

Randy, the man with the best 1970s feathered hair ever. Frequently wearing a Western shirt with snaps, tucked in tight like a military guy does; other times, just a white tank or tee. My uncle, who loved me like a daughter. His cup was always half empty. He was always worried that he wasn't enough and needed to be more. But, man, he loved fiercely and deeply. This led to the reality that he was always worried about those he cared for. He wanted them to be okay. He wanted to do for them, socialize with them. He would do anything for me. He used to tell me that he wished he was my dad. He loved going down memory lane, and he always missed the good ole days.

Sometimes I feel like we control our journey, and sometimes I feel like we are following a journey designed for us. Randy told me that there was no longer a cure, and he was going to be needing hospice, all while I was suddenly going to be near him.

He was mad at me; he thought I made the change for him. Maybe part of that is true, but maybe he was the vessel to get me to make the change for me. I don't know, but it worked.

Randy always wanted his son and me to hang out with him and have beers with him. We both did, but never together until the week that Randy died. I can still see Randy half-sleeping, half-enjoying the moment where his son and I became friends. We laughed, had Paglia's Pizza and Busch Lights. We played music—Randy's old, maybe some would call cheesy, music. The Flying Burrito Brothers is a band that I now know. Randy needed that night. His son and I needed it just as badly.

I was hoping Randy would give me a glimpse of heaven, and when he was dying, I was so certain of it that I would look and ask. I got the familiar grin, but nothing concrete. I asked him to visit me if he was able and to give me a sign once he got where he was going. For a while, I saw the same bald eagle flying over my car every day. Sometimes it was a nudge or a memory. But one night, it was a dream.

There was a crowd, and I couldn't get through the crowd to get to Randy. I could not see one face in the crowd but could see the crowd. They were in my way. He saw me and saw me working hard to get through all the people to try to get to him. He, of course, was taking care of everyone, and his crooked grin was the biggest ever. I kept trying and trying, and I wasn't getting any closer to him. He was waving at me. Also, maybe waving me off. It was good, though. I knew I couldn't get to him. And he knew I couldn't. Things were buzzing, and he was loving every minute of it. He was filling mugs for people and handing them out. He looked amazing. Same signature hair. Same grin. His eyes were so bright. He was younger. No worry. No frown or shoulder shrug that he did when he was worried. No shortness of breath. No pain. As he waved at me, he mouthed to me that he was great, and it was okay for me to go.

I am happy and teary as I write this. He hasn't visited me in a dream since. I miss him so, but know he found his heaven. Save a red bar stool for me, Uncle Randy.

A LESSON FROM
THE CARPENTER

I grew up in a rural community where you know, know of, or are related to everyone. Being a hospice nurse in our neighborhood places you in all those scenarios. It was no different with Sid, the toughest, smartest, hardest-working cowboy, carpenter, and family man I had ever met. Frankly, after taking care of him for a few days, I was scared to death of him. We say that your end-of-life journey tends to mirror your life. Sid fit that bill. He was large and in charge in all that he did. He was known for being the best at his craft. He was the head of the family and his business. If he had a thought, it did not stay in his head; all thoughts were to be voiced. Even if it meant you didn't like that hospice nurse coming into your home to provide care.

Days went on and trust developed. I grew to look forward to his stories and sense of humor. I fell in love with his family. I watched them rally around him, eat together, share memories, play games. I watched them tease and laugh and love one another. One of the community pastors visited and shared in the fun and banter as well. It truly was beautiful.

Sid was getting sicker, weaker, but still strong as an ox. The kids pitched in to help their mom and care for their dad. The grandkids were adorable; they were so comfortable together, cousins being friends, playing, and making up games. One particular game was hiding a little toy in Grandma's treasures and finding it. I learned to play the game Sequence with this family. Truly a remarkable time, and I was blessed to be their navigator and now friend to walk this road with them.

Sometimes we don't talk about the labor or work at the end of life before you go to heaven. That labor can present in many ways. Sometimes the end-of-life work can be misinterpreted for pain. It is so important for us that assist with navigating this journey to recognize the difference and support the patient's wishes for comfort and alertness the best we can.

I believe in my heart that so often, this is a time for the person to accomplish unfinished business. It might be a bucket list. It might be seeing someone. It might be personal work that only the person going to heaven can work through. It can even be reconciliation and making sure all is right in your soul. It can be a gesture to hand the baton to the person that will be taking over your earthly responsibilities.

Sid's story is so important to share because he had unfinished business. It just took us some time and misadventures to recognize. He was having discomfort, but we also figured out he was working. He was up and down, moving his arms in a very deliberate fashion. We worked feverishly to control his pain and restlessness. Then we had an aha moment. He was building his last work of carpentry, one we would never see this side of heaven, but he was building. We changed our dialogue with him; we supported him in his work. We allowed him privacy to do his work. His son handed him "tools." His eyes were squinted, his speech not always clear, but there were nods and pointing, directing. And then there was quiet and rest. He was done building and the restlessness was gone. It was shortly thereafter that he made his way to heaven. His family at his side just like they were for the entire journey. It was a job well done.

I earned a nickname in this home, but more importantly, I gained forever friends and a lesson from the teacher, the carpenter. Let the work happen. Hard work leads us to the fruits of our labor. Thanks for allowing me to be a part of your family. Love, Sally.

BACK TO THE GARDEN
WITH SOPHIA

"Sophia, can we talk about heaven and what it means to you?"

Sophia's deep brown eyes continued to take in all our conversation and stories, and she nodded slowly.

"Close your eyes and imagine your best day ever. Can you describe it to me in detail?"

Sophia squeezed her eyes closed tight, and she was quiet; then her eyes softened and stayed closed. Sophia was grinning ear to ear. "It's a sunny day. There is a breeze. And *purple* everywhere!" she exclaimed and giggled. "I am outside by my garden. There are dogs and puppies!" Sophia pauses. "Not five or even ten, no! There would be a hundred dogs—oh yes, a hundred!" More giggles. As we talked, Sophia shared her hope of getting to take care of all the dogs in heaven, especially the dogs whose owners haven't made it to heaven yet.

"Is that what heaven will be like for me?" Sophia asked with some tears.

"Oh, Sophia, girl. Here is what I can tell you. I have never been to heaven. But I get to take care of people just like you that give me glimpses of heaven. I have stories and beliefs, but I have never been there. Some people have talked to me about the music, while others have shared about the flowers and colors. Some people talk about the people and the angels. I have heard the words peaceful and amazing. I believe that heaven is so perfect that our brain cannot even comprehend it. What I can say is that I believe heaven is even better than your best day ever. Have you heard of the word *faith*? That's why we have faith—because we are choosing to believe in something that we haven't seen or experienced yet. Faith is amazing. Faith will help guide us to heaven."

One day when I arrived to see Sophia, her grandma was waiting at the door for me. "Sophia has been waiting to see you. She is so excited to talk to you that she is bouncing all over her bed!"

"I had a dream! I had a dream!" Sophia shouted while smiling as big as I had ever seen her smile.

I sat in silence and awe as I listened to this sweet little girl describe the dream she had been praying for. "I felt like I was floating or flying. It wasn't really either of those, but both of those. It is so hard to explain. It felt *so* good. I want to go back. I want to feel that way again."

"Sophia, please tell me more," I coaxed, sitting on the edge of the sofa.

"Oh yes, I could see so much. It was the colors—they were so bright! The white was the whitest white ever. I wish you could have seen how white and bright it was. And then there was the pink! The pink! *The pink!* It was the brightest, sparkliest pink in the entire world! If pink were a bright glittery light, that might be it. It was the best pink ever! It was the coolest!

"Can I go back? I want to go back," Sophia continued to exclaim with pure joy.

"Sophia, your dream sounds perfect. What do you think it was?"

"I think it was heaven. I wanted to keep going, but I couldn't. It was like when you said I will eventually have one foot here and one foot in heaven. Only both feet came back here this time."

Sophia got quiet again and said, "What I really want is to get better. I don't know why they can't find a cure."

We sat in silence together. We were teary at times.

"Sophia, I just want you to know that it is okay to cry, and it is okay to be sad."

"I don't want to leave my family. They are going to miss me and cry. I don't want them to be mad at me for going and to think that I wanted to leave them. I am afraid that I will miss them too and be sad that they aren't with me."

"These are the hard conversations. I am so glad we are talking and sharing our feelings. I know I don't have all the answers. I have learned a few things though. Sometimes your cure doesn't happen here with us. It happens when you get to heaven. Jesus is here with us now, and he will be there to welcome you home to heaven. You will get to see him in heaven. That's the super cool thing about heaven. No pain, no sickness, no worrying. Meeting Jesus and your grandparents face to face. Heaven is your perfect day every day. No time passes, so you won't even know how long it has been when we get there to be with you. I also want you to know that we will all be sad when you leave us. We will have good days and really sad days. But that's okay. It means that we love you."

"If I can't get better, why can't I just have both feet in heaven now?"

"That's one of the answers I don't know for sure. But here is what I think. Jesus picked you to be his special angel, and your job here with us isn't done yet. Maybe your job is to teach me something. Maybe it is to help all the kids at your school learn about Jesus and heaven. Or to teach us how to love and care for all the animals. Or to help your brothers or sister learn something extraordinary.

"Oh, I like that," Sophia whispered to me. She looked at her sister and brothers out of the corner of her eye.

"It means I am special. Did you guys hear that? I. Am. Special." She said it loud and proud, all while sticking out her tongue. Everyone giggled.

"It is also okay to laugh, play, and have fun doing the things you like to do. Like your parade. It is today!"

"I don't want to go to my parade. I am different now. I sleep more. I don't walk. I look different." Sophia looked away.

"Can I tell you a secret?" Sophia nodded. "When our loved ones do special surprises for us, like bringing us food or arranging trips and wishes, and in this case, a parade, it is sometimes more for them than it is for you. It gives us a way to celebrate you. Cheer for you and the life you have lived. It is also a gesture saying that we love you, and it is okay to go to heaven when you are ready. We will all be with you at your parade. Can we all go together and have some fun while making memories together?"

"Yes," Sophia said with her sly, crooked grin, "let's do it."

*****

"My parade was so much fun!"

Sophia smiled and shared stories about her friends and family all wearing purple shirts.

"Yes, Sophia. It was a perfect parade, and we got to celebrate you. Your family and friends had so much fun too!"

*****

"What if I get scared along the way?"

"Sophia, that's the answer I know for sure. Pray to Jesus to show you the way. Ask him to come into your heart and to shine his light for you to see. Also, pray and thank Jesus for all your blessings. Close your eyes and list your blessings, like your mom and dad, your grandma and grandpa, your brothers and sister, and of course, all the dogs! Remember, I told you about the man that sang 'Jesus Loves Me'? He needed to be reminded of his faith and that it was okay to look for Jesus. As it gets closer for your time to go to heaven, always remember those words and that song. It might help you when you are uncertain.

"I like that," Sophia said.

"Think of your perfect day. Imagine what heaven will be like. Like in your dream where you saw our new favorite color, heavenly pink."

Sophia smiled, and her eyes shined.

"Sophia, I love that twinkle in your eye and your bright smile."

"Like the lights in my garden, I will also shine," Sophia said with her famous grin.

"Yes, Sophia, you will forever smile and always shine bright, just like the lights in your garden."

ABOUT THE AUTHOR

Angie Wilson is a Midwest family girl and a proud wife, mom, and grandma. She is also a registered nurse who has spent the past twenty-eight years as a hospice nurse. Although her first job in hospice felt temporary, it ended up being her life's work. Angie shares that she feels hospice is her ministry, and she feels honored to walk on holy ground each day that she serves patients and families in this most intimate time. She has won numerous awards, including the *Times-Republican* Nurse of the Year, Hospice Pinnacle Award, and multiple quality and leadership awards. Angie also was nominated and selected to lead a hospice and palliative care team in Cape Town, South Africa, where she learned quickly that her modern medicine was not available, leaving her to rely heavily on the care of the mind and spirit of those in their final days.

Angie uses her experiences in hospice service and her infectious energy as a motivational speaker, speaking to leaders, professional organizations and boards, congregations, and community organizations. Angie has worked with world-class organizations to improve hospice quality and improve timely access to end-of-life care and symptom management at the end of life. Angie loves teaching new clinicians and leaders how to maintain the integrity of hospice service and provide the highest-quality end-of-life care. Angie lives in her hometown, Le Grand, Iowa, with her husband, Todd, and her two sons and their families.